Arthur Starter Book 13

# ARTHUR'S
## Tree House

by Marc Brown

Long tail Books

Arthur came home with his new Bionic Bunny comic book.
He couldn't wait to read it.

Dad was vacuuming in Arthur's bedroom.
"Do you have to do that now?" asked Arthur.
"I'm afraid so," said Dad. "I'll be done in a little while."

TUCKER

Arthur went to the living room.
“Watch me!” said D.W. “I’m practicing my new twirl.”
“I can’t,” said Arthur, “I’m busy.”

"Mom, can I sit . . . ?"
"Not now, Arthur," said Mom.
"I'm right in the middle of this."

Arthur went out to the backyard.
"Maybe I'll just sit out here," he said to himself.
Pal started jumping on him.
"Not now, Pal," said Arthur.

But Pal didn't understand.

Where could Arthur go?

He looked to the right.

And he looked to the left.

And then he looked up.

"I see you found a place for yourself," said Dad, who had finished his cleaning. "You look pretty comfortable up there."

BIONIC BUNNY
FREE
NEW!
BIONIC BUNNY

"Hey, what about me?" said D.W.

"Any branches left?" said Mom.

"This was a great idea, Arthur," said Dad.
"But I think we should make some improvements."

It took a while to get everything just right.

Once the tree house was done,
Arthur had a new place to go.

And so did his friends.

DARK BUNNY
CHIPS
TOLON

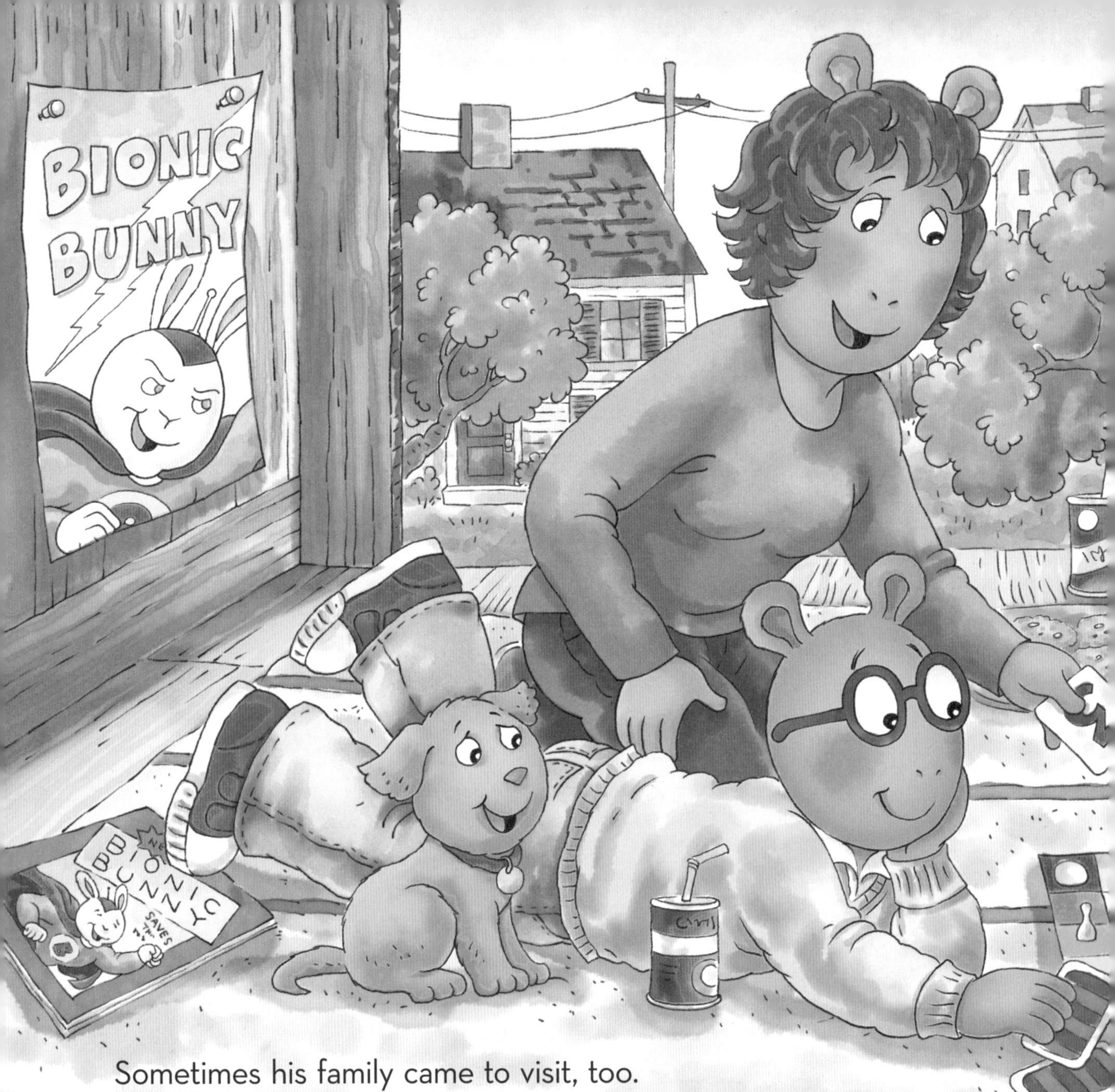


Sometimes his family came to visit, too.
Arthur was glad for all the company. But there were times . . .

when he still liked having the place to himself.